I Can Read with My Eyes Shut!

I Can Read with My Eyes Shut!

By Dr. Seuss

BEGINNER BOOKS A Division of Random House, Inc.

Library of Congress Cataloging in Publication Data:
Seuss, Dr.   I can read with my eyes shut.
SUMMARY: The Cat in the Hat takes Young Cat in tow to show him the fun
he can get out of reading.
[1. Stories in rhyme.   2. Reading—Fiction]   I. Title.
PZ8.3.G276Iae   [E]   78-7193
ISBN: 0-394-83912-9 (trade); 0-394-93912-3 (lib. bdg.)

Manufactured in the United States of America.   **50**

For

David Worthen, E.G.*

*(Eye Guy)

I can read
in **red.**

I can read
in **blue.**

I can read in
pickle color
too.

I can read in bed.

And in purple.
And in brown.

I can read in a circle and upside down!

I can read

with

my

left eye.

I

can

read

with

my right.

I can read
Mississippi
with my eyes shut tight!

Mississippi

Mississippi,

Indianapolis

and

Hallelujah,

too!

I can read them
with my eyes shut!

That is
VERY HARD
to do!

But it's bad for my hat
and makes my eyebrows
get red hot.
so ...
reading with my eyes shut
I don't do an awful lot.

And when I keep them open
I can read with much more speed.
You have to be a speedy reader
'cause there's so, so much to read!

You can read about trees . . .

and bees . . .

and knees.

And knees on trees!

And
bees
on
threes!

You can read about anchors.

And all about ants.

You can read
about ankles!

And crocodile pants!

You can read about hoses . . .

and how
to smell roses . . .

and what
you should do
about owls on noses!

Young cat! If you keep
your eyes open enough,
oh, the stuff you will learn!
The most wonderful stuff!

You'll learn about . . .

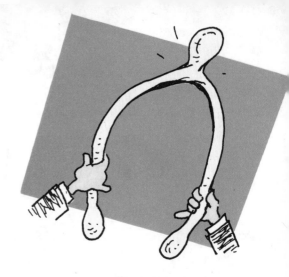

fishbones . . .   and wishbones.

You'll learn
about trombones,
too.

You'll learn
about Jake
the Pillow Snake

and all about
Foo-Foo the Snoo.

You can learn about ice.

You can learn about mice.

Mice on ice.

And
ice
on
mice.

You can learn about
the price of ice.

Nice ice
for sale.
Ten cents a pail.

You can learn about SAD . . .

and GLAD . . .

and MAD!

There are
so many things
you can learn about.
BUT... you'll miss
the best things
if you keep
your eyes shut.

The more that you read,
the more things you will know.
The more that you learn,
the more places you'll go.

You might learn
a way to earn
a few dollars.

Or how to make doughnuts . . .

or kangaroo collars.

You can learn to read music
and play a Hut-Zut
if you keep your eyes open.
But <u>not</u> with them shut.

If you read with your eyes shut
you're likely to find
that the place where you're going
is far, far behind.

WELCOME to WILKES-BARRE
DALLAS
SAN DIEGO
LAKE FOREST
SCHENECTADY
Bikes Only
DETOUR
NO EXIT
NO RIGHT TURN
LEFT
?
STOP
REST ROOMS 128 Miles
SALINA Kansas Birthplace of Curtis A. Abel 2376 Miles→
XYZ
ABC

SO . . .
that's why I tell you
to keep your eyes wide.
Keep them wide open . . .
at least on one side.

Dr. Seuss

...says that he had a hard time finding someone who would pay any attention to his first children's book. Happily, that never happened again. ...That book and the more than thirty others he has written since have all become modern classics.

The most famous of them all may be THE CAT IN THE HAT. This extraordinary story was so revolutionary in its impact that it created a new kind of publishing for children: Beginner Books, books that children could read (and delight in) all by themselves. With the Cat as their symbol, and Ted Geisel (as Dr. Seuss is known when he isn't writing or drawing) as their creative inspiration, *Beginner Books* and *Bright and Early Books* have helped millions of children discover what great fun reading can be.